BRAIN BOXING

RODNEY JOHNSON

authorHOUSE®

AuthorHouse™
1663 Liberty Drive
Bloomington, IN 47403
www.authorhouse.com
Phone: 1 (800) 839-8640

Published by AuthorHouse 11/30/2016

ISBN: 978-1-5246-5304-0 (sc)
ISBN: 978-1-5246-5303-3 (e)

Print information available on the last page.

This book is printed on acid-free paper.

Contents

ACKNOWLEDGMENTS

First, I'd like to recognize my mom and dad. Next, I acknowledge Randy Reed, Rebecca Reed, and my aunts. And may Aunt Minnie Jenkins rest in peace.

INTRODUCTION

*B*rain Boxing is a collection of fifteen short stories. The opening story, "I Saw It All," implicitly asks the reader the following questions: If you saw something horrific happening, would you tell someone about it? And if so, how long would you wait, and who would you tell?

In "The Night I Met My Doppelganger," the main character thinks, *Whenever I go out, I can feel the eyes of another person watching me.* He has that feeling you get in those dreams where you're being chased by a dog, and no matter how fast you run, you can never escape.

"The Girl Next Door" tells the story of a young man who falls in love with the young woman who lives in the building across the street from his. Her persuasive invitations slowly lead him to take a risky chance. In doing so, he gets the shock of his life.

In "Games Women Play," a woman plans to set her boyfriend up. Will he take the bait?

In "Three-Card Monte," two young boys help bust a known con artist who preys on innocent high school students.

The plot of "Six Days Left" has a young man strangely running into old friends, people he hasn't seen in years. He is haunted by the fear that the world is coming to an end. Is it, or is it merely that *his* world is ending?

Will the main character of "If You Only Knew" lose everything on account of a beautiful woman?

In "Twenty-One," a simple basketball game of twenty-one determines the fate of one player after the bet has been placed.

The employee in the eponymous story "The Employee" is, for whatever reason, shunned by former coworkers. Hoping to prove his loyalty to the company, he is tricked into performing a dangerous task.

In "Guilty Conscience," a man is haunted by the death of his wife. As he wrestles with guilt and grief, his life takes a tremendous turn for the worse.

A misinterpreted love letter tells of a fetish gone a little too far. Can the writer of the letter deliver? Passion and desire are played out in "A Love Letter."

A recently well-established young man awaits his trial after being caught in a compromising position. *All right,* he thinks, *ever have one of those dreams about cheeseburgers and you wake up hungry? You go to the refrigerator expecting to find cheeseburgers, but then you have the audacity to get sad because there aren't any cheeseburgers there.* This is the theme of "Oops, I Just Woke Up and Thought I Had Money."

I Saw It All

U lysses stepped out of his car and parked it in the vacant lot. Walking toward the small crowd, he was carrying a pistol in his right hand and was wearing a tight pair of nylon stockings over his head.

He approached the gray hot dog stand that was pushed up against the corner wall of the Burgess Juice Bar.

"Look! Over there," one woman said to her friend, pointing her index finger at Ulysses.

But her friend seemed as if she could care less. She didn't know what was about to happen. Ulysses leaned his back up against the cold brick wall, took a couple of deep breaths, put on a pair of latex gloves, and loaded the pistol before placing it in his shoulder holster.

After reaching the end of the brick wall, he peeked around the corner to see who was there.

It wasn't until he made it to the green iron Dumpster in the middle of the alley that Ulysses overheard three voices talking in the distance. They were coming from three people sitting on the roof of a car—two boys and one girl. He quickly recognized the voice of one fellow as he laughed. It was Felix, the same kid who had started this mess.

Thinking to himself, Ulysses edged closer and closer.

Water splashed under his sneakers as he stepped in the puddles made by that morning's rain.

"I hurt that kid bad!" one of the guys bragged. "You saw it, right?" he gloated, holding the girls' attention, until the small group of kids laughed out loud.

"Please!"

"Please!"

Even the girl wearing a pair of tight jeans with a rip in the seams laughed.

From his position behind the corner wall, Ulysses could see that the three people were so into their conversation that none of them had heard or even noticed him. But it was the girl who finally noticed him and screamed out first. Her two friends jumped; it didn't even seem like they were afraid. As a matter of fact, Felix had his head turned away, facing one of the side streets. Suddenly, he looked around and then stared Ulysses in the eye. Ulysses took one hand off the pistol and, with the other, pulled off the stocking. He wanted to be sure he was the last person Felix saw.

Shortly afterward, Ulysses walked over to the small group. Felix was crying intensely and shaking with fear. "Please! No! Don't do it! Please don't shoot me!" But Ulysses wasn't hearing it, not after what they had said to him earlier. Ulysses soon motioned Felix to get on his knees. But it was like Felix knew what was about to happen next, because before Ulysses could say a word, Felix was already on the ground with his mouth open wide, crying like a baby.

Ulysses began pissing all over Felix's face. Just when it seemed like it was over and Felix couldn't take any more humiliation, Ulysses did exactly what he had come to do. Quickly, he pointed the barrel of the gun at Felix's forehead and pulled the trigger. All I remember hearing was five pops and a loud scream. The girl jumped while the other guy ran. In seconds, the police arrived. As dark as it was that night, I could still see the billy clubs in their hands. Eight officers slammed nightsticks across Ulysses' bloody head. Some people ran; others watched.

All I thought was, *This is a terrible thing.* I stood at the front entrance of the juice bar, where all this mess had started about twenty minutes ago.

Felix had squared off with Ulysses. It seemed as if the scrawny Ulysses hadn't had a chance in the world challenging Felix. Through it all, I had to give him credit for going up against him the way he did.

Ulysses had been in the bar earlier, hanging out with that girl, when Felix came over with his friend. I bet if they were up against him, they'd have run like church mice. But Ulysses didn't run, not this time, even though Felix was famous for cock blocking, and for starting trouble in the nightclubs with his friends.

I'm serious—it's not like they didn't have competition; they just liked to use their weight against smaller guys like Ulysses. And like naive pushovers, the so-called intuitive girls more often than not carelessly fell right into that bi-curious trap. I remember telling one of the girls once, "Those guys—they don't even like you. He's just trying to prove a point."

Then she asked why I didn't do the same.

"What? Cock block?" I said.

"Yes," she replied.

"I just think it's for sissies, if you know what I mean."

Blame it on the weather or the atmosphere, but right

near closing time, everyone was very anxious to leave. Crowds of people lined up like in a school cafeteria.

It popped off. Shattering bottles of Heineken and Smirnoff Ice clapped against the brick wall, clinking like church bells. It looked like one of those old Wild West flicks or a scene from the video game "Street Brawl." The fat one, Felix, slid through the crowd like a gorilla let loose at the zoo.

Bouncers chased Ulysses down the first flight of stairs. The walls shook as their heavy bodies ran across the floor.

I don't even know what that kid Ulysses had done this time, but whatever it was, it was bad.

About twenty minutes after everyone finally made it outside, the crowd gathered around the hot dog stand to see the messy outcome. Felix had beaten Ulysses to a pulp. Blood spat from his mouth, his nose, and wherever else Felix had hit him. I'm serious. It splashed all over the large crowd. Still, the onlookers didn't move or even attempt to stop the fight.

I saw it all, standing beneath the branches of a tall tree.

There were even two girls beside the gray hot dog stand. One of them spoke to her friend, pointing at Ulysses as he had stepped out of his car earlier.

I doubt the other girl knew what she was saying at the time. One of them noticed bright blue and white lights flash from a distance after hearing five shots quickly ringing out.

Then a small crowd of officers—maybe eight, if that—came out of their squad cars with nightsticks in their hands.

THE NIGHT I MET MY DOPPELGANGER

What if someone was checking you out, eyeing your moves, sizing you up from the rear, and mimicking every move you made? Sounds flattering at first, doesn't it? Yeah, I know. The mere thought of someone else digging your style almost turns you on.

Perhaps it would leave you thinking, *What did I do? What am I packing? What's so attractive about me?*

But hold on. This person is the same sex as you. That's right. So don't even go there—at least not yet.

Listen. Just listen. What if I told you he's been following you around for some time now? He's gotten your routine down to a science. It's like he's been sweating you with a vengeance, and he's been doing his homework. He knows where you go, when you go, who you're with—and why.

No! No! No! I wouldn't do that if I were you.

In a fearful panic, I—my name is Phoenix—reached for the .38 Special to place underneath the rug in my gray pickup. *Now that's more like it, more of an appropriate response. Think clearly,* the voice said back to me. *Give it some thought, seriously. What's the last thing you remember?*

5

Well, lately I could feel the presence of another person watching me. That sudden uncomfortable feeling started to curdle in the pit of my gut, like the night I went out to the Café nightclub. What shook me off of my feet when it happened was that the doorman wouldn't let me in after seeing my ID.

"No!" he said, shaking his head at me. *Why?* did cross my mind as I watched him flare up, growing red in the face.

Then he claimed he had seen me there the past weekend starting up some sort of a ruckus.

I wasn't willing to pursue the matter further—I mean, the night was young and there were plenty of other places to go. At the same time, I just wanted to know why.

I'm the last one to start, let alone pick, a fight.

"You must have me mistaken for someone else," I said to him before leaving.

But he insisted, relating that I was the one who had started the fight.

The man standing beside him had looked at the picture and then back over at me, nodding his head. "Yes, that's him." In no time, I was in the next town over at a spot called the Bruges Juice Bar. Oh, and there had been a certain incident at work involving a customer who asked me tacky questions. Saying that she had seen me before, she asked if I had a twin. I told her that I didn't, that I had lived here on my own for a long time. My parents moved away to Florida when I turned seventeen. I had no family here.

But this particular woman insisted she had seen me, or a relative of mine. Not meaning to be rude, I replied, "No!"

But she continued to insist, even going so far as to say,

"That's wrong for you to not go with your parents. You must have been a bad child."

"I'm grown," I said back to her. It even got to the point where I just said, "Stop! Leave me alone." Now honestly, if I had heard this information from someone a few years ago, it would have amused me or grabbed my attention in a good way, but such was not the case this time. If I wanted to be serious enough about it, along the lines of paranoid, I'd recall at certain times a few guys—three, maybe five at the most—would show up unexpectedly at my job, of all places.

Now, I know working at the fish market can get crowded at times. And several customers come back for more. But these few fellows were always together at certain times. They would toss their heads up in the air at me as if I was someone they knew or they had something on me. See, I'm a loner. Why? Because I know people. I also know that one thing that's more powerful than sex or money is control. Everyone has to have something on someone.

Not me. I was carefree. Clean people didn't even like me because I was so clean.

I wouldn't care if I died so long as I knew that no one had ever had anything on me.

That was why I freaked out like I did when I found out someone had been following me. *Me? Why?*

Things started to get a little more intense almost a week after I went to get my gray pickup from the Jiffy Lube station on Allen Street. Given my situation, I remain parked for a while. I was thinking that perhaps it would help divert the crowd's attention away from me.

I even remember getting a ticket for leaving my .38 underneath the rug. I guess the mechanist told on me. I can recall telling the officer what had been happening to me lately, the stalking and the threats.

He said I should have reported the crime. After I displayed my gun permit, he let me go.

I figured that if I kept quiet about it long enough, things would go back to normal soon enough.

But in order for me to put a stop to this, a complete stop, I had to keep my eyes open. I couldn't afford to be blind or let my emotions get the best of me. Flames like this one didn't just burn out by themselves. According to the state of things, this fire had been brewing for some time now.

I went out as usual to see for myself what I was really up against. This time I was a little more attentive, which made me slightly vulnerable. I would open my shocker just a little, which was partially dangerous. See, I'd never been an offensive fighter before. And to get this person to stop—I mean, really stop—I had to fight offensively.

Making a simple suggestion wouldn't work, as unfortunately we were not living in a utopia society. Besides, he was lying in the cut. A deep cut, very deep. I didn't know who he was. For me to pull him out, I had to antagonize him.

There was one night I'll never forget. I went out to the Café, the local spot where friends of mine would go after work. I was standing at the bar listening to music when I noticed a young lady calling me over with her eyes. Hesitantly, I stepped toward her, pointing to my chest to make sure she was talking to me. She nodded her head yes, so I lifted my index finger, suggesting that she wait.

Immediately she shook her head no, insisting I go over right away. After enough poking and prompting from her, we finally introduced ourselves. "Hi," she said. "I'm

Jenny." I hadn't even paid her any attention because she was so beautiful, out of my league. For a second, I couldn't concentrate.

She had jet-black hair, chocolate brown skin, and big bright eyes. Yes, Jenny was hot. As time passed, we got a little more acquainted, but before I knew it, it was time to go.

I walked outside with her. As we approached the steps, she surprised me by asking for my phone number. Reluctantly I gave it to her, providing she didn't let anyone know she had it. As she stepped away, she said she would call me Monday night.

I wasn't sure she would call, but it turns out that she did. On 8:00 Monday night, my phone rang. Jenny and I talked for hours that night. I even lied to her. "No, I don't drive," I said, being under the impression that if I drove, it would bring me unnecessary attention. Besides, if she was still interested after hearing that, it would mean that she was tenacious, a winner, the kind of woman who'd stand by her man. So how's that for knocking down two birds with one stone?

"After I pay off the rest of my bills, I'll get a car," I said, figuring that the mess with the stalker would be cleared up by the time Jenny and I were a couple.

While at work, I could vividly recall that woman from the shop, the customer who was always asking me strange questions. I learned that she worked at Dunkin' Donuts across the street. Anyway, she stopped by for a few things, saying that she was on her break and couldn't stay long. She even asked if I had gotten my truck back or if someone else was using it.

"I could have sworn I saw a gray pickup leave the parking lot earlier today. It looked so much like yours," she said. "I was even going to say hi. If I wasn't working at the time, I would have." This woman and I had resolved our differences some time ago.

Later that same afternoon, my cell phone rang. I got the feeling it was Jenny.

Turns out it was her. She asked if I wouldn't mind going out with her and a friend later. I agreed, suggesting we slip over to the Café.

Jenny was on her break during the phone call. She said she'd be punching out in the next hour or so. "Take your time getting ready. I'll call a cab to pick you up when you get off."

Promptly, as I expected, my cab arrived. "Where to?" the driver asked, but before I even said a word, he was driving.

Funny, I saw Jenny right away. We stared each other in the eye for a moment as I stepped out of the taxicab.

She giggled, shrugging her shoulders at me. I smirked, thinking, *Perfect timing. How ironic that we run into each other like this.*

She was with her friend, the girl she had spoken about on the phone. I recognized her face, but I wasn't quite sure where I knew her from.

"Hi, I'm Phoenix," I said, reaching out my hand toward hers.

"Tammy," she replied, shaking my hand and looking over at Jenny.

I started to feel a little exposed, like I'd felt earlier when those guys showed up in the fish market. But this time the feeling was very uncomfortable. It was beyond fear and to the point of anger and annoyance, almost like feeling another person breathing down my neck.

As much as I wanted Jenny, and as pretty as she was—like Gabrielle Union, or the principal's daughter on *Boston Public*—I couldn't help but feel uncomfortable. No matter how much I wanted to open up to her and have fun with her, I couldn't.

We all got into Tammy's car. I sat in the backseat, while Jenny rode shotgun. Later that night while driving back to the Café, Jenny turned around to face me so we could talk.

I could see Tammy's reflection in the rearview mirror. While I was listening to Jenny's conversation about how she liked working out at the gym, she reached underneath her seat and pulled out a bottle of what looked like Bacardi Silver Raz or Smirnoff Ice. She asked if I wanted a beer.

"No thanks," I said. "I don't drink."

"What do you do?" she asked, a flirtatious twinkle in her eye.

"Make love," I said, drowning into her beautiful eyes.

"No, silly! I mean bad things, stupid!" She laughed, watching me as I reached in my front pocket for a cigarette.

"See, I'm a smoker," I said, asking for a light.

"That's no fun!" she replied with a frown on her face.

My eyes glanced back over at her friend. "Oh, I'm sorry. What's your name again?"

"Tammy!" she said while taking the next exit. It took us perhaps four minutes to get the Café—that is, after I convinced Tammy to stop by my place to pick up my truck.

Jenny shouted out, "Liar. I thought you said you didn't drive."

Deciding that I might like to have her come with me, I said, "Come on! You want to come?" It seemed that before I asked, she was already out of the car and in my truck.

Jenny and I seemed to be hitting it off pretty well that night. I even felt like I was in there.

"What's that?" I heard her scream out.

"Oh, nothing!"

Her face looked serious for a second. It was then I knew her foot was touching my .38.

Later on that night, I felt uncomfortable again, that same feeling flaring up in the pit of my gut.

"We'll be right back!" Tammy said as she and Jenny started heading toward the restroom.

I went out to my truck to move my .38 from beneath the rug and stash it inside the passenger-door panel.

Little did I know that apparently not one guy, but all five of the guys who were following me earlier, were there.

Once I was back inside, I looked across the room and could swear that I saw Jenny speaking with a group of strange people. I thought I didn't recognize them until I looked closer. One of them was the same woman from Dunkin' Donuts who would ask me those stupid questions.

What I wanted to do next could have changed the whole outcome of that night. I didn't care, though. Like I said, I had to put a stop to this. *I had to.*

I walked directly into one of those guys who had been following me. Jenny and Tammy were somewhere else in the bar at the time, so they didn't see it. Right afterward, the guy pushed me back.

I let the anger simmer for a while so as to pump up my adrenaline, which would eliminate any guilt or remorseful feelings I might have had about my behavior. As I said, prior to tonight, I had never seen this person before. *Never.* But I knew he was the one who had been following me. He had to be.

The guy and I stared directly into each other's eyes for the first time.

Ironically, the same guard who had mistaken me for the person who had started trouble in the bar last week was there. I found it strange that he didn't even attempt to stop the fight. As the guy and I fought, the crowd quickly slipped out of our way, watching us like dirty old cowboys fighting it out in the Wild West.

The guy took a chair and slammed it on my back. I fell to the ground, grabbing his ankles on my way down.

He fell, bumping his head on an iron pole. The tension grew as we punched and kicked each other, and slammed one another around like rag dolls.

If I were to step out of my flesh and look down at myself, I wouldn't have recognized myself. The behavior I displayed was distastefully odd.

I punched the guy while asking, "What do you want? Why are you following me?"

He didn't say anything; he only smashed another beer bottle on my head. In a way, I wanted him to deny that he'd been following me. If he did deny it, I'd believe him. That way, all that had been happening would be the product of my imagination. I'd embarrassingly lose the fight, risk getting beat up, and that would be that.

But it wasn't that simple. No. He was the one who'd been following me. I had to fight, even if it meant getting knocked around a little. That's how serious I was; that's how violated I felt. I was actually willing to risk losing a fight and getting beat up right in front of a bunch of strangers so that I would no longer have some dude following me around and spying on me.

As we wrestled, he screamed out at me, "Why'd you let it happen? Why?"

I had no idea what he was talking about. He began to run down the first flight of stairs, apparently heading for the parking lot and his car.

I chased him. You could hear the tires of my pickup screeching on the pavement as I raced through the parking lot. I jumped on the highway, heading toward the next town. I ended up passing the guy. That's when his car purposely tapped my bumper twice.

While I was pulling over to the side of the road and reaching into my door panel for my gun, it turns out he was doing a similar thing.

Back on the road again, I looked into my rearview mirror. Before I knew it, my truck was spinning out of control. He had shot my back tire! My truck flipped over three times, smashing into the guardrail.

The guy got out of his car and walked over to my truck to look me in the eye. He said, "I hate you! That's why I did what I did to you. That's right, I hate you." He was speaking in a loud voice. "You have nothing. You're nothing. Now I can live the rest of this life …"

THE GIRL NEXT DOOR

She lived in the next building across from mine. I could see her from my back porch.

She'd sit in her windowsill gazing into the day. At first I wondered if she knew me, whether she'd seen me before, and if she knew I was watching her.

Prior to noticing her, I had been going out more often in spite of the bad area I lived in, not to mention the fact that I was a fairly private person. But there was something about her that caught my attention right away. It was almost like—and I'm not quite sure if I'm saying this right—I could feel myself falling for her more and more every time I went outside.

I liked watching her idly swaying her long, soft, pretty legs back and forth, back and forth. Her face was quiet, innocent, and as soft as pure affection. I wanted to know who she was and where she came from, or at least who was she waiting for.

I had just gotten home. Shortly after stepping back into my apartment, I convinced myself to stop thinking about her. I was afraid of making a fool of myself. She'd probably catch me looking at her and then confront me about it, and then I'd be forced to admit that I'd been watching her. Then she'd tell me to stop. But I wouldn't have denied it, no. See, that's the thing: she looked that good, as crazy as it seems. I knew it was strange. Call it pathetic if you want. But I ran with it, telling myself she noticed me and felt violated at the thought of my presence.

It wasn't even twenty minutes later when something caught my attention, urging me to go back outside. Something in my gut was—or maybe it was that my desires were—getting the best of me. Whatever it was, it was strong—strong enough for me to heed it.

So there she was, facing my direction. It startled me, like the feeling you get when a dog is breathing down your neck or when you are a child and are caught red-handed taking a cookie from the cookie jar.

Now I know I told you she was shockingly gorgeous and I crazily admitted to spying on her, but what if it wasn't like that at all? Let's say, for the sake of just saying, that perhaps it was her who was watching me, 'cause, really, she could have been. But let's be practical now. This girl was *hot*. What would she find interesting about a guy like me?

Throughout the time I'd been watching her, I gave her no inkling I was digging her—or did I?

After a few days had passed, I noticed she wasn't there.

One day I remember leaving for work at 8:00. I needed to empty the trash, so before leaving I went out back. That's when it hit me that she was gone. I thought about her on my lunch break, anxious to get back home to see her. She wasn't there.

About another week had gone by. I started to feel disappointed, figuring that she'd never lived there and was just a visitor passing through. Or maybe she was a former tenant who had found another apartment.

Shortly after coming to my senses, I realized this was radical and asked myself why I would feel this upset over a stranger. I could have smacked myself for that.

Anyway, I opened my blinds just enough to see if she was outside. I wanted to be sure.

Momentarily, I slipped out back and looked over the balcony. There she was sitting in her window seat as usual, as if she had never left.

And it was then, after all the days and weeks, and maybe a month, that she threw what looked like a smirk or a wink in my direction. I gulped in stunned surprise. Then I jumped, tripping on the wood banister. I screamed "Help!" all the way down the stairs.

O→←○→•○•←○←→O

Early the following Monday morning, the maintenance man, the landlord, and some detectives searched the premises for clues. A young man's body lay dead on the pavement beside the building. He had broken bones, including fractured vertebrae in his neck and a cracked skull.

The crime scene investigator said, "Look at the eyes. They're facing up there." He was pointing in the direction of the apartment the young woman was supposed to have lived in.

"Does anyone live there?" one of the detectives asked the landlord.

The landlord quickly shook his head no. "There's never been anyone living there."

Another detective began to speak, saying, "Because it looks like he was too much of a coward to jump. Check out how the bones are broken. This wasn't a suicide, was it?"

GAMES WOMEN PLAY

I was hip to her game from the start. The funny part about it is that I let her get away with it. She did it right in front of my face.

Have you ever liked someone so much that you couldn't end the relationship no matter how hard you tried? That was the case for me. I couldn't break things off with her.

What intrigued me most was that she was so calculatingly clever about our whole affair. I can honestly say it kind of turned me on.

Lisa would suddenly grow distant from me whenever he called. I will use only the pronoun *he* to refer to him, because I am still in such disgust about their whole affair. I couldn't—excuse me, *didn't*—even want to know his name. The mere sight of him upset me.

I heard them talking on the phone for some time one night. I didn't know exactly what they were saying, but the tone of Lisa's voice told me she was engaging in a conversation with a man she was romantically involved with.

Now, normally in a situation like this, I would leave— leave the relationship, confront the woman, or burst into a violent rage. But I didn't do any of those things, 'cause, like I said, I liked her.

I remember her accusing me of liking Sheila, her best friend. I don't know everything, but I've been around long enough to know that girls like Lisa carefully select their friends. For instance, Lisa knows she's an attractive girl, but she'll never let you know that. On the other hand, there's Sheila. Well, we'll just say she looks okay. On a scale of one to ten, she's a six. Okay, a six and a half.

Then there's Trish, the high-class type of snob every girl has got as a friend. Now Trish is almost a seven in my book, but if you ask her, she'll tell you she's a healthy nine, close to a ten. But get this: my girlfriend and her best friend, Sheila, are always talking about Trish like she's some kind of icon or something. "Trish this. Trish that." God, does it ever stop? The two are forever comparing themselves to her, adjusting their priorities to fit her standards. Everything's always about Trish. Now this seems odd to me, because boys stop this type of behavior when they are about six or seven years old, whereas girls continue it well into adulthood.

Anyway, I was talking about Sheila, my girlfriend's best friend. Well, she was the one who introduced Lisa and me. We'd hit it off from the start about ten months ago. Everything seemed to be going fine until this mess started. I'll explain that later.

But looking back on it, I think that Sheila could have set this all up herself, under the persuasive influence of Trish, of course.

Lately I'd been opening my eyes a little, paying attention to the games girls play. To say this one had kind of gotten me confused is an understatement, seeing how much I liked her. To think she'd try to use that "You don't listen to me enough" line on me. It just didn't pan out for me anymore, especially coming from an intelligent girl like her.

One day I was waiting for Lisa to finish doing her laundry. "I'll be right back," she said to me before shutting the door to my apartment, taking a tall basket of dirty clothes with her. There was another load in the washing machine.

Sheila would have probably gotten away with what she'd done if it hadn't been for the fact that Lisa and I had been together so long. See, girls usually cheat well into the relationship, whereas us guys do it toward the beginning.

I was sitting on the couch resting after a long day's work. The doorbell rang twice before I answered it. To my surprise, it was Sheila. She burst in, her face drenched in tears.

"Lisa's downstairs doing laundry," I quickly told her, not wanting to get involved and urging she speak with Lisa. I just wanted to relax and didn't feel like going through all of this mess with Sheila. Besides, it was a girl thing, something girls should be talking about—*not me.*

Without warning, Sheila quickly grabbed me. She had tears in her eyes as she threw herself at me, burying her face in my chest. "He's awful," she said. "He's a loser!"

I had no clue what she was talking about, at least not at first. But then I realized it was probably Garnet. "Who?" I asked, a word I shouldn't have said.

"The guy I've been seeing for the last month is married," Sheila cried hysterically. She had left the front door open.

I stared out through the front entrance, looking at the banister's railing. As I began to focus my attention, I could hear Lisa's footsteps confidently stomping up the first few flights of stairs.

"Why can't all guys be like you?" Sheila said, stopping for a brief moment, her arms around me.

That was when Lisa stepped into the room carrying a basket of clean clothes. Just then, Sheila said softly, "You're the best. I always liked you."

Shocked at what she had said, I was pretty sure Lisa had heard it too. I was hoping she'd come over and dispute it. Instead, she dropped the laundry basket and screamed at the top of her lungs, "What!"

Shocked as all hell, I couldn't say a thing. I tried explaining, but no matter what I said, Lisa didn't believe me.

Lisa and I fought for weeks after that. She claimed she'd stopped hanging out with Sheila. I was actually beginning to be convinced she was serious. I mean, Sheila never once tried to defend herself.

Just days ago when I happened to be passing by the place where Lisa worked, I overheard giggling in the background. It was Lisa, Sheila, and some dude from the gas station—not Garnet, but someone else.

I had intended to reconcile the relationship between Sheila and Lisa, as Lisa seemed distraught over the whole thing.

One voice traveled through the walls, saying, "I wasn't sorry, or maybe I was." It was a woman's voice.

I had bought Lisa five cream-colored roses. Perhaps I did it to console her.

Moments after, I saw Lisa and Sheila standing in the cafeteria line talking. I overheard Lisa speaking fondly of Garnet.

That's when it hit me: Sheila and Garnet had had

nothing together. That so-called altercation that happened back in my apartment had just been a setup.

Lisa had conjured up this whole stunt. If it hadn't been for today, I'd never have known. She said it all standing in line. The words crawled out of her mouth as easy as vomit from a sick child. She was talking about Garnet. That's right, it was Garnet.

That was all I needed to hear, but she couldn't see me or know I was listening. I just left it at that.

THREE-CARD MONTE

"Keep your eyes on the diamonds, the king of diamonds. That's it, the king of diamonds," the dealer said, looking around at the crowd as he shuffled three loose cards on a folded sheet of newspaper.

The competitors were playing a game of three-card monte in front of a slowly growing crowd, ten people at the most. "Where's it at? Where's it at?" the dealer asked excitedly when almost half the crowd reached out to grab the middle card.

The finger of one girl who looked to be about sixteen years old even touched the piece of newspaper sitting on his lap.

"That one!" she screamed. Unfortunately, the fellow's bet was already placed.

You could see the four loose twenties in his hand as he reached out to grab the card. "That one?" the dealer asked.

"Yes!" the fellow said.

"Are you sure?" the dealer said, tipping the card over. It was the king of diamonds, just as he thought.

In what seemed to be the middle of the game, the dealer reached in his front pocket and pulled out a wad of cash about an inch and a half thick. The bills were large—fifties, hundreds. There was nothing smeller than a twenty. He slowly began to count out each bill in the palm of his hand, saying, "One, two, three …"

Three hundred dollars. He gave the fellow with the orange shirt three hundred dollars right in front of the small crowd.

"Keep the change," the dealer said before starting a new game.

Two young boys in the back, one fourteen years old and the other sixteen years old, chattered to one another, saying, "He's giving all his money away." They were talking about the dealer because the fellow in the orange shirt could have played that hand over and over again. It took him only twenty minutes to make out with a good eight hundred dollars, easy. He had won each hand he played.

The fourteen-year-old called up enough nerve to place a bet. He had only $10 for the week to pay for transportation, food, and whatever else he needed until Monday. If he lost this hand, that was it! But if he won, like the fellow who had just played, he would have an extra $10 in his pocket.

The boy's friend, whose name was Pete, tried telling him not to play, but the boy who wanted to play, whose name was Devin, brushed him away, insisting on taking this outrageous chance. He didn't care that Pete had tried to influence him not to place a bet. All Devin could see was $20 resting in his front left pocket.

After the dealer flipped the card over, the crowd booed, whispering, "Ooh! He lost." Everyone was making all kinds of noises. They were heckling and making snide remarks, saying things like, "He could have beat that hand"; It was that one"; "I saw it"; and "That one. That one!"

That was when the girl, the sixteen-year-old, stepped up, anxious to play. Her name was Beverly, she said. She had only $30 on her. She, like, literally leaped over the wooden benches to place a bet. "That one!" she shouted. Excited, she was touching the first card, which was hanging off the edge of the newspaper.

Suddenly the crowd grew intensely quiet. The dealer asked, "Where's your money? For this game, you got to have money to play. If you don't got money, you can't play. I'm trying to eat.

"That man right there," he said, pointing over toward Pete, at the fellow in the orange shirt who had just won $800. "He just took all my money," the dealer complained.

"I have money," Beverly shouted, pulling the three tens from her purse.

The dealer tipped up the newspaper toward her. "Pick one!"

Beverly reached for a card, but this time she changed her mind. It was a red card, one that looked like a royal. Just as she felt that vigorous tickle in the pit of her gut, thinking it was the king of diamonds, she found out that it wasn't. In fact, it was the king of hearts.

She asked the dealer if he would show her what her first pick was. Sadly, it was the king of diamonds.

Pete and Devin walked away, heading toward the bus station. "I almost had it," Devin said.

"I told you not to play," Pete reminded him.

Their bus arrived shortly. Carelessly thinking he had some money left over, Devin dug into his front pocket to find the money to pay his fare. "Over here!" his friend Pete shouted, waving him over. "I paid your fare," he said, an uncomfortable expression on his face.

That evening, Devin thought for hours of ways he might retrieve his money. Nothing came to mind.

By Tuesday, Devin had begun to feel the loss of his money, knowing that he wouldn't be getting paid until the following Monday. But he managed to scrape together just enough change to get himself through the next day.

To make matters worse, Pete didn't show up for school the following day. This made Devin very nervous. Knowing he would have to walk home, he attempted to call his mom on his cell phone. When she answered, he said, "I'm going to stay over Pete's house for a little while." She said that would be all right as long as he was back by 6:00 p.m. "Okay," he answered quickly, not wanting her to know he'd lost his money the way he did.

After getting off the bus in the center of town, leaving a good fifteen- to twenty-minute walk, Devin thought back on what had happened at the bus stop on Monday. *I'll never do that again.* He was dripping sweat from his forehead. *Pete was right. Those guys were just scheming against us for our money the whole time.*

He began counting the days in his head, feeling desperate and anxiously thinking of how he would get to school on Friday. Pressed for time, he took a shortcut through the vacant lot and walked across the playground. That's when he heard shots burst out from a distance, coming from the alley up ahead. It was two rounds in sets of three. All of a sudden, Devin saw a gray Chevy van pull up, its tires screeching by him, as if the driver were watching him.

The van backed up and turned around. It literally

left faster than it had come. It tore through sets of traffic lights before it finally slowed down. Then the driver looked through the window and stared Devin in the eye.

Devin froze. Have you ever fallen asleep on your back and then found once you awoke that you couldn't move? Well, Devin felt like that. By the time the van left, Devin realized something serious had just happened.

Running frantically through the lot to see what the van had left behind, Devin discovered, like a smack across the face, a man lying in a ditch and drenched in blood, the same man who had ripped off the crowd at the bus station. He was lying there lifeless, wearing the same orange shirt. "Dead," Devin said.

Devin tugged at the guy, prompting him to sit up, but the man had seriously passed away. Just as Devin was going to call it quits and call for help, he saw a huge stack of cash slip out of the man's pocket, all hundreds tied tight with a rubber band. Devin quickly slipped the money into his own pocket. After speaking with the proper authorities, he called his friend to tell him what happened.

"Maybe the girl they ripped off did it? Maybe she got some friend of hers to settle the score."

Six Days Left

I thought it was kind of odd running into Jill the way I did. I hadn't seen her for so long. For her to just pop up like that on the spur of the moment was strange, seriously strange.

Now don't get me wrong. Charles was flattered by the unexpected reunion.

Come to think of it, prior to last week, he'd been running into people he hadn't seen in a while. Take Sue, for instance, who used to shop at the same grocery store for years. Charles went out with his friend Dave one night, and Sue happened to be there with her friend Jill. Shortly after the two were introduced, Sue shook Dave's hand. Jill spoke softly, saying, "This is Dave.

"Dave, this is my friend Sue," she said in a humorous panic. The two got acquainted with one another pretty quickly.

I must admit, as much as Charles liked Sue, he had never given her an inkling that he was interested. Charles knew Dave, and the girls knew Charles, but Dave didn't know the girls.

It wasn't long after their meeting that Dave engaged in a conversation with Sue. That was when Jill began talking to me. I totally dreaded having a conversation with her, so

I hardly listened to her words, which sounded to me like, "Blah, blah, blah!" Nevertheless, I wanted to be around her.

She kept talking until she caught my attention with the news of a local girl's death, saying that the story had caught her attention while she was flipping through the *Sunday Republican*. It was a shock to us all. I think I even knew the girl. She used to take the bus with me. They say she lived in those high-rise buildings over on Cleft Street. I didn't even know her name, not until Jill mentioned the story. In fact, if I was correct, Dave said he saw her last week as we were driving by the bus stop on Grinas.

It didn't hit Charles until a few seconds later. He would have given her a lift, but there were too many cars behind him. Besides, she didn't know Charles. If he'd have picked her up, she probably would have thought he was up to something. That's what Charles thought as he listened to Jill talk about how she had tripped on something while running in her apartment, saying she had fallen down three flights of stairs.

After Charles had gotten home from work the next day, Dave happened to stop by. He said a young woman was looking for him. Dave had told her to leave a note, but she insisted on seeing Charles in person.

Charles had even run into his sixth grade teacher that week. That's when things started to get a little strange. Dave was walking through the Larense apartment complex at about 11:30 that night. It was the second week of September to be exact. There was no hurry to be home, so he took his time.

As he walked further up the road, he said, he heard songs from an old church at the bottom of the hill. They were old gospel songs, one of which sounded very familiar, something to the effect of, "I'm gonna be just like him. I'm gonna be just like him. I'm gonna be just like him when he comes." Repeatedly, over and over, again and again, the singers sang. They wouldn't stop singing that same old song.

Dave never understood what it meant, but it sounded strange, which is probably why the song startled him.

Now Charles was not one to watch the news often, thinking, *It just doesn't make sense sometimes. I mean, it's always bad news, headline after headline.*

Charles could remember growing up listening to his teacher say things about the end of the world, telling the students that they had better join the church or else they would miss being redeemed at the end of the world. And it wasn't just any church they should join; it was the teacher's church.

As ironic as it sounds, Charles ran into Dave later the next day. Dave looked startled, anxious—a little too anxious, Charles thought. He started to rant about something he had seen on the news. "It happened!" he shouted. "It happened!"

"What?" Charles quickly asked, having no idea what Dave was talking about.

Charles looked at Dave as if he had never looked at him before. Dave began ranting about it being the end of the world.

It wasn't long until Charles realized what Dave was telling him.

"Think about it," Dave went on. "Everyone's affected by what happened. Those planes that just crashed? That was the cloud. Everyone saw it. It says he's coming back with a vengeance."

"Dude, you're sick," Charles said, interrupting him. "You need help."

As if Charles wasn't even there, Dave kept talking, giving the impression that he really thought it was the end of the world.

Dave said he felt like he couldn't take it. He even burst out into tears. "My whole life's been a lie," he said, quickly rushing home.

Once Dave got home, he pulled out a gun from beneath his dresser and then shot himself in the head.

"Can you believe it, Jill? Can you believe it?"

"Guess everyone's got their own end of the world," Jill said with a tear in her eye. "A lot has changed. A lot has changed."

IF YOU ONLY KNEW

I got the call on my cell phone at about four that afternoon. I was gliding down the highway, screaming along the interstate to reach the exit that would take me to the trailer park.

It was Maxine. She was in a frantic rage, talking about how she needed directions and saying she was in town and needed to see me.

This was all happening too fast. I didn't know what to think, asking myself, *Who is Maxine?*

Then it hit me. Maxine was the girl I met in the mall three weeks ago. I had never expected her to call.

She was beautiful. I guess that's why I forgot about her.

"Listen," Maxine said. "I need your help."

While she was talking, I thought, *Why would she think to call me of all people? I'm serious. Three weeks have passed and now she decides to call?*

"Do you have a place for me to stay for a while?" she finished asking. She sounded shy but also like she was in some serious trouble. Immediately I thought, *Yes,* especially considering the tone of her voice. Let's not forget that I'd had my eye on her for some time, almost as long as it took for her to call me. Besides, kicking up enough nerve to give her my phone number the way I did weeks ago had been exhausting enough. Spending time with her on one day would keep me satisfied for almost a whole week. She would look at me in this strange but sexy way that threw me off balance a little.

Come to think of it, sometimes she had come to visit me on my break and spend ten, twenty minutes. I was nervous at first when she did it. I could have sworn I had blown my chances, but surprisingly she stayed, telling me to finish my work and saying she'd wait for me at the mall entrance.

That's what perhaps had given me the courage to give her my number when I did. We spoke to each other that day, and she told me about her last relationship, how she had gotten married at a very young age. Listening to her, I got the impression she wasn't happy. But the stories were so compelling that I couldn't stop listening. Above all, she was gorgeous. I never imagined things would end up like this.

I headed toward my exit. I put on my right turn signal to switch lanes when I asked, "Where are you?" She didn't know, saying she was lost. "See if you can read one of the street signs," I said.

"Riverdale Road!" The static in my cell phone started to pick up. All I heard her say was "River," but I was so familiar with the area that I knew exactly where she was.

"Stay right there!" I told her. "Don't move. Park somewhere. Wait for me!"

Before I hung up the phone, I had her give me a landmark. I knew that Riverdale was a highly industrial piece of property, one of the main attractions in the area.

"What's that?" she asked.

"A commercial residence!" I screamed back at her. "Or a

Burger King, McDonald's, Shell, Citgo, a popular franchise, anything. A restaurant, a gas station—whatever is closest. Stay right there. Don't move!" I realized the minutes on my cell were running out.

She screamed, "There's a plaza coming up on my left. I can see PECO. Ah, there's a Staples and an Old Country Buff—something. I can't read the rest."

I pulled up in front of her car in a parking lot. We spoke. She told me she was leaving her husband after four years of marriage. She was sick of his not paying enough attention to her. I didn't feel compassion for her 'cause I'd heard that line before. Plus, I liked her. She could do a lot better than that. I thought she was giving me a hint to hook up with her or something.

We spoke for some time that afternoon. She claimed she was on the run and had no other place to stay. I offered to help. "I don't have much, but you're welcome to stay for a while. Follow me."

I got in my car and headed back toward my place. *Funny.* I couldn't help but wonder, *Why me, of all people? Why me?* But I had no time to contemplate the decision. We arrived at the trailer park within ten minutes.

She opened the trunk of her car. There was luggage, clothes, baskets, and all kinds of things stuffed inside.

What the hell is that? I thought. I noticed the expression on her face. It seemed that she had been planning on moving in with me, depending on if I said yes. What if I hadn't answered her call, if my cell hadn't been on?

She followed me up to my trailer. The wood squeaked as we stomped up the steps together.

Now thinking back on it, I shouldn't have ever told

her the trailer was mine. Doing so was something I'd later come to regret.

"Listen. I have just one rule, and that is that no one is allowed in here while I'm gone." She seemed to take heed to what I was saying.

The first two months went by like a breeze, so smooth it felt like weeks. Things couldn't have been going any better.

In spite of all the effort I put in to making Maxine feel comfortable, and in spite of how much I'd stressed to her not to let anyone else in my house, she let someone in.

I clearly remember going to work Tuesday night, seeing as she wasn't working. I was sent home early that day because business was slow. When I made it back home, I noticed there was someone else in my house. I could have sent Maxine away then. I should have, but I was too tired to say anything.

It was the calls at night that bothered me. A strange man called looking for her. At that point, my feelings for her had slowly started to decline. I tried brushing it off at first, but then it hit me: *I'm not getting anywhere with her.* As much as I liked her initially, I wasn't impressed with her. Slowly I lost all interest.

She started showing up with lots of cash, not tips from a waitressing job but oodles of dough. I'm talking fifties, hundreds. I'm sure you know what I was thinking, that I was letting my feelings get the best of me.

Word got around in the neighborhood that Max was turning tricks. Back in June, I had been living alone anonymously. Now it was September, and the whole block had their eyes on me, wondering.

○✦┼◇•●○•●◇┼✦○

"I remember picking her up at the bar one night. She'd been drinking a lot, so I had to cover her up a little. That's when it happened."

"What?" another inmate asked.

"I swear, I didn't even have sex with her." With that, I was finished speaking.

Three dudes sat on the jail bench listening. Frank, the guy wearing a net stocking cap, passed me his rolled cigarette. "I wonder who was pimping who?"

Another fellow spoke out, almost as if he was confused or something. "You trying to tell me that she wasn't your girlfriend?"

"Nope! Not only that, but we never even had sex. And Detective Crane arrested me!"

"But you wasn't her pimp?"

It didn't matter. As long as we lived under the same roof, I was guilty—guilty by association.

The judge had slammed his gavel, giving me three years.

Two years later, I was walking down Main Street when I saw a cruiser flash its high beams at a woman. "Hands on the car!" the officer screamed forcefully as he brushed his hand up Maxine's naked leg. She turned her head, her eyes level with the officer's badge, which read, "Crane." "Where's my money?!" he shouted. Then he shoved her up into the trailer where they both lived.

TWENTY-ONE

D oug shook his head at Fish, saying, "I want out!" He was holding the basketball in his hand and standing in the middle of the court.

The court was atop Fish's three-story penthouse.

Fish laughed at first, not taking Doug seriously. The two were taking a quick breather between sets in a tiring game of twenty-one. "You're making so much progress. Are you sure you want to quit? Look how much money you're making," Fish told him as though trying to convince Doug not to quit. Doug was one of Fish's best pushers. He would buy steroids from Fish, preferably boosters. Doug sold the drugs out of his sports shop. The agreement worked out pretty well financially, considering how much rent Doug paid on the property.

"Everyone does it, all the locals." In fact, Fish had just hooked Doug up on this new Canadian connection worth 47 G's. Now that Doug was pushing for him, this $47,000 could easily turn into $94,000. That's how much juice Doug had on campus.

It would hurt the business an awful lot if Doug left. Fish become irate, screaming, "Where's the rest of my money?" Then the two men stood up and began playing again.

Doug stalled for a while, passing the ball and thinking, *How the hell am I supposed to get out of this one?* The tension between him and Fish grew intense. What Doug was about to say would surely send Fish over the top. "I still have a hundred capsules left."

"You know how much that's worth?"

But before Fish could say another word, Doug interrupted, almost begging. "But you said I could leave whenever I needed to, no strings attached."

"Is that right?" Fish said snidely. Then he interrupted himself as if having a bipolar mood swing, screaming at the top of his lungs, "Quit?! Quit?!" His voice had gone from a calm hush to a fearless rage, which only left Doug feeling awkward and out of place.

Seeing a crooked look on Dave's face gave Fish that much more incentive. "Tell you what. If I win the next game, you stay till you pay back all my money. If you win, you can leave. Just like that—no strings attached. Cool?" Fish nodded his head.

"Cool!" Doug couldn't believe what he was hearing. "No strings attached?"

"Nothing!"

Doug and Fish played for hours that afternoon. Doug dribbled the ball across the court, making point after point. It seemed as though Fish didn't have a chance. With only two shots left in the game, Doug could think of nothing other than getting out for good. In less than a moment, he had swished two baskets, meaning that he'd reached twenty-one. He shouted. The ball bounced toward Fish.

Doug jumped around in excitement, coming to stand at the four-foot-high railing. "I won! I won!"

Fish bounced the ball back to him, saying, "But it's not that simple. Yeah, you won. You can leave."

Doug took two steps back. Fish stared at him then like he was without worries. Then he quickly punched the ball. It slammed into Doug's nose. Fish watched the blood drip from the side of Doug's face. Doug staggered for a few steps, jerking his body back.

Doug finally lost his balance, screaming as he fell over the balcony.

Fish watched him fall, saying, "You didn't get the rest of the deal, did you? If you win, you can leave—but don't ever come back."

Fish laughed as he stepped away from the railing, saying, "You really thought you won, didn't you?" Shaking his head, he thought, *I had to let you win, you perpetual loser!*

THE EMPLOYEE

"I'm not going to let his attitude ruin our chances," the young woman said harshly.

Jerry had just asked the supervisor for a new shirt. "No!" the supervisor replied after having him stand up so she could see the shirt he was wearing. "That fits fine," she shouted. She wanted to charge him an additional twenty-five-dollar application fee.

"You sound like the feisty type," the supervisor, whose name was Sam, said.

"Feisty?" Jerry said, surprised and shaking his head no. The tone of her voice made him believe that she didn't think he had the money.

As soon as she walked over, Sam, not even knowing any of the interns, insisted on assuming she had something on Jerry. He said he had gone to Berkshire High since the tenth grade. Sam had gone to Belmont. The two schools had been rivals for a very long time. But Sam and Jerry hadn't known each other.

Sam eventually stepped out, leaving the four applicants alone to eat lunch.

Jerry and a few others had been laid off from work for sixty days and had had to reapply to get their former jobs back. The state had taken over the company. Now there was a fifty-dollar fee to take the test for the job. Not only that, but also there was no promise they'd be hired again. Not to mention that Jerry had even contemplated leaving months before he was laid off.

I'll never forget it, Jerry thought. *It was a Tuesday afternoon after picking up my check. I was thinking that I needed to get something else, a different job. I worked so hard and so much but couldn't even pull in a lousy three hundred dollars a week.*

Back then, looking at his $215 paycheck, Jerry had felt angry that his rent was at risk of being raised another $50. Add that to the cost of his car insurance. And then there was the thought of that grimy old hotel he may have to stay at again. Thinking he'd never go through that experience again, he was back to the horrific drawing board.

Now Jerry had to compete for a job he'd already had. *It's not enough to wake up and go to the job, but now we have to work to get it. I guess now I know what it means to rest in peace.*

Eating his half-empty plate of cold french fries, Jerry could feel a stern nudge on the back of his left shoulder. Todd whispered to him, "Cool down!"

"I didn't do anything!" Jerry replied. "She came at me!"

Surprised, the others—Spencer, Tiffany, and Carla—stared in shock. They had all heard the conversation.

Later, Sam came back into the room to show them around the new building.

Jerry, Todd, and Tiffany decided to work maintenance, while Carla and Spencer would work security.

"Here's the trash compactor," Sam said. You could hear her voice echo through the hall.

Spencer leaned over Jerry's shoulder and said something about her breasts.

Jerry just blew it off like it was nothing, but Spencer persisted until Sam turned around. She screamed Jerry's name. Everyone in line stopped moving.

"If you don't want to be here, leave," Sam shouted out at him.

Jerry didn't know what to say. Spencer was acting as if he'd had nothing to do with it.

It wasn't long before Jerry caught on to what was happening. He settled the incident for himself. He felt as if what he was going through was an interrogation, not an interview or orientation.

Jerry thought of the last conversation he'd had with Todd, weeks before.

"It's almost a shame, the running around we have to do for these large companies," he'd said to Todd.

Todd had replied, "It's not like we get paid enough!"

Jerry had said, "I just hate how you have to do all these cartwheels. It's like they're shooting bullets at your feet and saying, 'Jump, jump!'"

"Man, listen, if I have to walk in the bitter cold, freezing rain, you name it, I will. But what else am I supposed to do?"

"Everyone has to work," Todd said. "If you don't work, you don't eat. It's as simple as that."

It was getting close to late afternoon break time. Sam decided to let Jerry and Todd work the assembly line for the time being. At a quarter to three, Spencer called Carla into the back room.

Sam happened to be at the trash compactor, waiting. As she opened the Dumpster, Spencer passed her a huge wooden log, which she began to shove down the caboose. She even had to take off her shoes to get leverage.

Encouraging Carla to participate, the rest of the group egged her on. She didn't seem as interested as the others did, but not because she felt sorry for Jerry, as she couldn't stand him either.

By the time Todd got there, the alarm system sounded off.

Jerry quickly left his station, dashing toward the back entrance. He saw the others quickly shove the log inside the compactor and yell, "Help! Help!"

Not exactly sure what was going on, Jerry attempted to get involved.

"There's a cat stuck in there!" Carla screamed. "Help us get it out!"

Jerry went to the compactor to assist in getting the cat out. All of his coworkers screamed loud.

Then it dawned on him, but it was way too late.

Todd, of all people, shouted out, "Shut the lid!"

Spencer pushed the big iron door closed.

Jerry even tried grabbing Todd's hand, screaming out, "Todd! Todd, no. Help me! Please!"

GUILTY CONSCIENCE

It was an accident, really it was, but honestly, between you and me, I wasn't sorry. If I could change anything about it, I wouldn't.

Clarence breathed a huge sigh of relief while listening to the popping wood as the Larense apartment complex burned. He didn't even know where the fire had started.

It was an intense moment as Clarence held his wife's hand and listened to her screams for help. Twice she cried, "Save me!"

Then Clarence released his grip. She held tight, watching him as if she were puzzled. She knew he wasn't trying hard enough.

He could hear the firewoman behind him saying, "Move. Get out the way," as the ceiling began to collapse.

Authorities later said there was nothing he could have done. One even pulled Clarence aside. She draped a wool blanket over him.

"Who was she?" the officer asked.

"That was my wife, Lisa," Clarence answered, sounding sad but relieved.

He and Lisa had been married for only three years, but he was completely fed up with her already. He couldn't stand the constant nagging and complaining, and the tedious prompting and poking that women do awfully well. The two of them had briefly gotten into it just a few days ago. Lisa was upset that Clarence wouldn't let her know where he was all the time.

Guess it's not because we fought, Clarence thought, sighing and thinking that what had happened was awful. *Some say we're never happy unless we're miserable, and that misery loves company. Or maybe we're just selfish people who'll never be satisfied. What an awful alternative death is, though.*

Clarence had read somewhere that all the problems we have just get us ready for the next—whatever that meant. In his opinion, what gets to you is the super reminding you of your overdue rent, or the boss threatening to fire you if you're late one more time. In Clarence case's, it was his place being set on fire. Now he felt that he was somehow responsible for his wife's death.

His mother had always told him not to be so inviting to women. "They're bad too," she'd complain. "Clarence, just be a little more selective. You'll find the right one."

What started as a minor rude awakening and a nightmare had caught his attention. It was a vivid dream of Lisa. Images of her operatically crossed his mind.

This happened often. It even got to the point where he simply couldn't take it anymore. Clarence eventually moved away.

He saw these images even when he was at work, during his lunch break.

He was working as a janitor part time for a company call Safety. It had been the only thing available at the time, so he jumped on it. Having moved to make a fresh start, he was fortunate to find a place so soon. It was a small efficiency for $500 a month.

It's almost a shame, Clarence thought. *I should have figured she'd break it off with me a long time ago. And I—well, after her treating me the way she did. She'd cut herself off from me as well. But why did things have to end up like they did?*

You know that how fast your hair grows is partly dependent on how much dust gets in it. Take two people with the same amount of hair and, let's say, a three-month period, during which time one is told to wash their hair every day and the other is told to wash their hair three times a month. The one who washes their hair every day will have less hair after the three months is up, seeing as humans are made of dust.

Take problems, wrongdoings. They have to happen to us, and we have to commit wrongs against each other in order to grow. After all, we're born in sin, aren't we?

Clarence thought back to the time when the super showed him around the apartment at Larense for the first time. It wasn't the best neighborhood in the area, but it was suitable for him, seeing as he'd had to move inconspicuously.

Two vacancies were available, one upstairs and one downstairs. He picked the downstairs apartment, only because the neighbors upstairs were exceptionally loud.

"Is there a way I can have my name removed from the doorbell system?" Clarence had asked.

The super laughed as if it were a strange request.

Clarence quickly took that as a no, but he insisted, threatening to forfeit the deal if she didn't comply.

After getting settled in, he disconnected the buzzer in his apartment and took the batteries out of his smoke detector.

A few months had gone by. He went to take his car into the shop for a tune-up. This would interfere with his work attendance, as he would have to take the bus for the rest of that week. While his workplace was in Prize, the next town over, the distance was still a good thirty minutes by car or by bus.

His boss put the heat on him about being late so often. That was ironically good, seeing the stress Clarence had been under concerning his wife's death.

One of Clarence's favorite parts of the day was when he was driving alone in his car, when there were no questions, no obligations, and no one to answer to.

He thought about Lisa one night on his way home after getting his car fixed.

He remembered feeling sort of responsible even though he hadn't killed her.

It's not like I wished the fire on her. Sometimes people wish pain on another person, but this was different. It's just that maybe if I'd tried harder, I could have done something, Clarence thought after making it inside his apartment. He sorted through his mail only to find a memo from the super saying that if he failed to come up with the rest of his rent, he'd be forced to leave.

That was bad, but it wasn't devastating. He'd just make up the hours at work and then pay his balance by next week.

The following days were colder than normal.

Clarence had been scheduled to be at work at seven that day. He remembered hearing people on the news saying not to leave the heat or the radio on in the car while it was cold, as doing so may drain the battery.

He took the bus, so he didn't get to work until eight. His boss did not want to hear his explanation. She fired him.

There were a few other places he had been looking into before getting settled in that town. He called a few of those places, Big D's for starters, which was a local department store. Turns out they needed a night janitor. After setting up an interview for the following Thursday, Clarence thought that he would get the job.

On the Tuesday night before Clarence's interview, he was taking a hot shower. Steam filled the apartment, sparking the live wires in the doorbell system he had disconnected earlier. Little did he know, that one simple event would be the thing to set off an awful chain of events.

Apparently while Clarence was sleeping that night, those wires kicked up just enough spark to set flame to the walls. By the time Clarence realized what was happening, it was way too late. The fire had already consumed a good half of the building. The ceiling of the upstairs apartment had begun to collapse.

This was very similar to the situation in which his wife, Lisa, had found herself. There was one difference, though: this time, not even a fireman was around to help.

Clarence screamed, "Help! Help!"

A Love Letter

I t was a hot summer morning toward the end of July.

I could recall hearing her say, "We were meant for each other." Soul mates, she called us. I was flattered but not quite amused, because that's what they all say, at least in the beginning.

Toward the end of the relationship, it was more like, "I can't stand the thought of you. Just looking at you makes me hurl. You disgust me!"

That's why I learned to take everything women say with a grain of salt. Claiming they're interested, they try to stroke your ego in some way, only to later rub it in the dirt like a rag doll. So when a man's feelings get hurt, who's to blame? I think a man who lets a beautiful woman determine his status, stamina, or whatever you want to call it is fooling himself. It's kind of like spitting in the wind— it just might blow right back into your face.

But no, honestly now, let's be frank. I had to give Heaven a little more credit than that. You see, of all the women I'd dated or let have their way with me, she was the only one who was easygoing and who was on another level. *Maybe that's why I'm still thinking of her like this.*

Older than I, she taught me a lot. She spoke vividly of

her childhood and told me that she had felt an absence of affection growing up.

I'm sure there are a lot of people you meet who would make prime candidates for one of those early morning talk shows and, if given the chance, would jump at the opportunity. But not Heaven. No, Heaven was a lot better than that. What we had was perfect—to me at least.

She was discreet and understanding. She even cooked for me. I remember the first time we made love. She had come over to my apartment and brought a plate of food for me. I was dressed in a white T-shirt and navy blue pants. I hadn't planned on her bringing food over, but she did. It was unexpected.

I shut the door behind her after welcoming her inside. She had worn a long purple gown. After she handed me the plastic plate, she stepped into the kitchen.

It was really hot out that day. From the sitting room, I said to her nicely, "Come out here and have a seat." I hadn't realized that what she was wearing was revealing until she sat beside me in the love seat. Soon after she had seated herself, we curled close to one another.

We were like two constrictors basking in the East African sun. Smelling each other's bodies got us more excited by the minute.

By dusk, long after I had finished eating the food she'd brought, the blinds over the windows cast a tall shadow across the east wall. The reflection off the shimmering brass finials on the lamps made the image of a cross appear on the end tables. This made the room look like a room in one of those Marilyn Monroe flicks filmed in the 1950s.

Heaven rested her head on my chest, nestling deeply

into it. She began to brush her hand across my frail abdomen without permission, lifting her neck to see if I was paying attention. Then she began to unfasten my pants. It was the smell of her breath that quickly got me aroused.

She kissed my chest, slowly working her way down to my lap. I felt her glide up and down the side of my body. The whole idea of what was going on threw me for a loop. Just having a strange woman in my place, an older woman at that, turned me on. It was sexier than sin itself. I imagined her as a babysitter, a teacher, or an older boss of mine!

I guess that in any other situation, we'd have been apprehensive upon meeting each other. Perhaps apprehension is what brought things to this point.

O⊁┝⌀∙O∙⌀┝⊀O

It was a call late Friday afternoon. "Help! Help!" a faded voice shouted.

It had been three weeks since I'd seen Heaven. Almost a full month had passed. Just as I was about to call it quits, I faxed her a letter. And then the phone rang.

It was Heaven, saying she needed to see me—and fast. "We have to talk," she cried.

"I can't come now," I said to her. "The earliest I can get there is tomorrow."

"No," she said. "This is an emergency. I need to see you right now." I could hear the panic in her voice.

It was then that I proceeded to get in my car and drive over to her place. But by the time I got there, she was gone. I had knocked on the door and received no answer. After waiting a while, I felt it was safe to leave, figuring she was playing some kind of game.

On Monday afternoon, a few days later, I was on my way home to check my messages and see if she had called. After I got there, a detective showed up on my doorstep with a picture in his hand. "Have you seen this woman?" he asked.

"How do you know her?" asked the officer who was standing beside the detective. I hadn't even answered the first question. I felt as if my heart would leap out of my chest.

Thinking of the last time Heaven and I had spoken, I thought, *Maybe when she said it was an emergency, she wasn't playing.*

The officer confirmed my suspicion, saying that Heaven had been attacked.

Quickly, I suggested that the police speak with Heaven's ex-husband, a guy she'd talked to me about.

"Is she all right?" I asked the woman detective.

"We'll keep you informed," the two answered as they stepped away.

Thinking about the things Heaven and I had done to each other in the past got me wondering. For example, I recalled the last time we made love, which was also the last time we had gotten into a fight. She was upset with me for not showing up on time, complaining that we hadn't been spending quality time together like we should. Then she said it wasn't in her best interests to see me again.

If she were hurt, hurt bad, I wouldn't be able to live with myself. I couldn't call the hospital, because I didn't know if the police were wondering if I, not her ex, had done something to hurt her. That is, I didn't know where I stood as a suspect. As ambiguous as our relationship was, I liked her.

Still, considering the last time we made love, I concluded that I'd go to jail willingly for her. That's how foolishly I was in love with her.

Thinking of the talks Heaven and I had and of our fight a few days back got me wondering if her ex-husband had found out about us. *Maybe she still loves him and used me to get back at him,* I thought in a panic, *or maybe she's looking for attention.*

A few hours after they'd gone, the police arrived at my doorstep again, except this time they were using the letter I had written as evidence of my romantic involvement with Heaven. Apparently a judge had granted them a warrant to search my place.

In no time, they placed me in handcuffs. One of the detectives who had traced the laptop to me even made a comment about my not resisting. He said, "This is the first time I've met a guy who is willing to go to jail."

After a bit of prompting and pleading on the officers' part, I finally decided to confess. The officer who said it was me who committed the acts eventfully confirmed that Heaven had died.

That was when I broke down. "It was me," I said, sinking my head down into my chest and feeling horrible.

○➤┝⊂▶•○•⊂┥◀○

One of the guards opened my cell. He told me I had a phone call. He escorted me off the bench, my feet shackled and my hands cuffed behind my back as he walked me down the long hall.

I saw the phone hanging on the bare wall. I picked up the receiver.

"Hello?" The woman's voice sounded raspy, as if she had just awakened. I had so much going on in my head that I didn't even know it was Heaven. But it was her.

"Hi," I answered, shocked but sad. I wasn't trying to imply that I was upset with her. I was just confused about what she had said to me earlier, how she felt it wouldn't be wise for us to continue seeing each other.

I didn't say anything for a few seconds.

"I'm sorry," I said, with a tear crawling down my cheek. It seemed that those words leaped out of my mouth before I had even thought them.

"Why are you crying?" Heaven asked.

Sniffing back my tears, I grabbed a hold of myself. "I didn't want to hurt you. You told me to do it. What I wrote in that letter was just a figure of speech. But it wasn't even that. You really got hurt!

"I'm sorry," I said again, crying over the phone.

"I know!" Heaven said.

"When the police asked me, I really thought it was your ex-husband, because they didn't speak to me until after the fight you and I had."

"I would have contacted you earlier, but I just couldn't." Then she cut off our conversation to say she had money for my bail.

I went home from jail that night, as Heaven had dropped the charges. The following month, we were engaged. And we have been living together since.

Oops, I Just Woke Up and Thought I Had Money

It was 10:30 in the morning, a sunny early July morning. What made this day more shocking than the others was—well, I was rich. Filthy rich. I had more money than I had ever imagined.

It had started on a Monday night, if I recall correctly. I was in my penthouse bachelor pad just about to turn in for the evening when I thought, *I'll make a withdraw from the bank first thing tomorrow.* I was anxious to do so. Approaching the end of the second quarter, I'd sold a large piece of condemned property for 193,000 tax lien certificates. The money was automatically deposited into my account.

I'd still have a good $430,000,000-odd dollars left. I was thinking about the vacation I'd been planning to Australia for the following week. It left a good taste in my mouth.

After my alarm clock went off, I wasted no time getting out to my car, a 2004 cranberry-colored Infiniti Q50 with dual exhaust pipes and cruise control.

I was cutting through traffic and racing down the side

streets until I was suddenly stopped at a red light. Not only was I on Clinton Boulevard, but also this was one of the junkier parts of town. And wouldn't you know it, a bum came walking over, approaching me from the side. Quickly, I looked in the other direction. *Tunnel vision,* I thought. *If I can't see him, he can't see me.*

But I was wrong. The bum even tapped on my windshield.

"See ya on my way back," I said. I then motioned the guy to move, as my light had turned green.

It was about a quarter past eleven when I got to the bank. Shuffling through my wallet for my account number, I pulled out a sheet of paper from beneath a paperweight on the courtesy desk. It read, "Sorry, we're out of withdraw slips. Please feel free to use the scrap paper."

Thinking I must have left my information at home, I glanced over my shoulder to see if I recognized any of the tellers. I didn't.

As I walked out of the bank, I couldn't shake the feeling that something wasn't right. *She didn't even count out the money to me. She just placed it all in a bag.*

I headed back to my car. As I was driving through town, I turned down a side street.

Looking in my rearview mirror, I saw a line of unmarked cop cars tailing me. Reluctant to pull over, I assumed they were my personal security, seeing how much money I was carrying.

I looked at the clock on my dashboard. It was 1:25 p.m. The digital display blinked twice. I turned into my parking lot, parked the car, and got out with the bag of money hanging over my left shoulder.

In the blink of an eye, everything changed. I felt different, like a new person. But then a policeman hollered through his bullhorn, "Freeze! Drop the bag!"

I knew what was going on—exactly what was happening.

Reality struck clearer as I took each backward step.

He was a plainclothes cop with a gun in his hand, and that gun was pointed at my face.

"Put your hands on your head! Fold your fingers together! Now move slowly my way!"

It was then that I awoke. I'd just had one of those dreams, a dream where I was rich. The truth was that I had no penthouse. The truth was that I lived on Clinton Boulevard.

Still partially in the dream, I was thinking, *Man, how the hell am I going to explain this one, not only to the police but also to myself?*

Oh—the plainclothes cop was undercover. He was the same man I had thought was a bum. See, I never had $430,000,000. That teller in the bank read my note and assumed I was holding up the place. That's why she gave me all that money like that. I dreamed the whole thing. It was one of those dreams everyone has from which they awake thinking they have money.

SWSH

All you could see was Jason's tall body laid out on the floor. He was covering his head and shaking like a fearful child in the fetal position. Blood covered the surface of the bathroom floor. He was in terrible shock. People ran, women screamed, and everyone was watching. Ugh.

As the paramedics cleared the entrance, the DJ stopped the music.

By now, Jason's face was turning blue. He was losing blood and losing it fast. Doc couldn't say what the outcome would be. All they knew was that this was a terrible chain of events. One kid even regurgitated, saying, "Imagine the guy who has to clean this up."

Lora and Jason had stepped out of the nightclub that afternoon. Lora began explaining to Jason how her relationship with her new boyfriend, Felix, was going. Jason pretended to show interest. He abruptly interrupted her. "Let me have a light," he said. Lora began to dig between her breasts for matches.

Waiting with a cigarette pressed to his lips, Jason was flattered by what she was telling him. He interrupted her again, asking, "Well, how come you didn't go out with me?"

"Because you weren't quick enough!"

He thought about Lora's answer. He had felt she wasn't serious enough for him. Apparently Felix felt that Jason was posing a threat to their new relationship. Lora even said that Felix questioned her about her relationship with Jason. He wanted to know what kind of friends they really were.

But at the pizza shop about a week and a half ago, after Lora and Jason had first met and exchanged phone numbers, they talked briefly, getting to know one another. It seemed as if she was closely engaged with Jason when Felix's crew drove by in a hooked-up-looking white Honda Civic.

"They are screaming out of their windows and showing off like clowns," said Jason.

But Lora seemed to be pretty impressed. As the two continued talking, Felix's crew crawled into the pizza shop together, four deep. The car engine was still running, as they'd left a guy at the wheel. Lora could have totally forgotten about Jason at that point.

She abruptly interrupted, saying, "Oh, he's so cute!"

Then she followed Felix out of the pizza shop and got his phone number. Jason decided to cut off contact with her at that point.

But later, while Jason was walking back to his car, he had to see for himself. He brushed up against Lora with a full-blooded erection, squeezing her close in a soft embrace.

He stared into her eyes for a brief moment. There was nothing.

And now it was a week later, and the two of them were standing outside a nightclub.

"So, you're trying to tell me," Jason spoke out, "that you liked me first?"

Lora nodded her head as if to say yes. "Your face is

better-looking. Your stomach is cut." She then giggled, saying, "And you're so big."

"You're silly," Jason answered.

"Why?" she asked.

He didn't say anything after that. He just continued smoking his cigarette, until Jill, Stephanie, and Sue walked up to the nightclub. The three passed by grinning flirtatiously while staring Jason in the eye.

"Why? Why?" Lora shouted out, watching him totally disregard her as if the two hadn't spoken a word to each other that night.

To make matters worse, Jason was falling sinfully into Susie's eyes. The two even kissed as they stepped up to the front of the nightclub together.

It couldn't have been any more than forty-five minutes later. While the four young men circled the nightclub in that white Honda Civic, Jason and Susie walked into the bar together, laughing it up and having a hell of a time without a care in the world. They began kissing and rubbing against one another.

Meanwhile, Lora was upstairs, oblivious to her boyfriend and his three friends.

By now it was 11:30. Three of the young men, leaving Felix behind, walked into the nightclub together. One went upstairs. The other two stayed down in the barroom, casing the place looking for Jason.

"Is that him?" one asked the other.

"Looks like him, yep," another answered.

One stepped away to order a drink while the other ordered the perfect attack.

"Stay right here!" Jason told Susie. "I have to pee," he

said, whispering in her ear. Seconds later, the two young men followed Jason into the bathroom. One had a bottle of Coors; the other, a Bud Light. With almost perfect rhythm, the bottle of Bud smashed Jason on the back of his head.

Quickly Jason reached his hand up to the back of his head to touch the wound. The second guy grabbed him from behind. The two tussled for a brief moment, the younger man winning, making Jason submit.

Jason screamed. The other guy cracked his bottle over the segment urinal and then grabbed Jason's manhood, cutting it off with a *swsh* sound.

All you could see was Jason's tall body spread-eagled on the ground.

IN A PROCESS OF TIME

When he first introduced the opportunity to me, I was, I have to admit, a little more reluctant than I was tempted. June was the boss of all the security guards who worked in many of the nightclubs, bars, and taverns throughout the area.

He insisted, begging me. "Just this once? You'll never get caught."

While well into the conversation, I realized I was in way further than I should have been—into the relationship, that is.

Now June wanted me to stick up a kid named Adrian for him. Adrian worked at the hardware store part time during the week and security on the weekends.

But what made this job bad was that I didn't know Adrian. At least not like that. I mean, I'd worked with the kid a few times, but aside from the job, he was a stranger.

I guess June had caught wind of his wife's messing around on him with Adrian. If you ask me, it was bound to happen sooner or later, considering how June paraded Lavira around like a trophy, or more like a prized dog on a leash.

June was one of those dudes you just couldn't say no to; he almost always had an offer you couldn't refuse. I mean, look at this. He was offering me a handsome amount of cash—under the table at that—just to rough up some kid I hardly knew. And even I didn't know if it was done intentionally or not. But coming from June, it might have been intentional, because just to be dirty about it, he'd arranged for the hit to happen right near the hardware store—in his own house.

Pulling me aside, June said, "Here's twenty-three thousand. Meet me at the hotel two days from now. I'll call you before anything happens. Do whatever you have to. I'll take care of the rest."

I can remember seeing the money for the first time. I didn't know what to think or what to do.

No, I'd thought the first time he pitched me the opportunity. *I can't do this.* But now, looking at all this cash …

It was Wednesday, the day after. I went on a job with Adrian at Café's nightclub. He was boasting about how good Lavira was in bed. I just brushed it off at first. Then I realized he was trying to get on my good side, which wasn't easy considering what I had to do.

He even mentioned spending weekends out in the Heights, a rich section of town where June owned a few houses, Now if I were one of Adrian's friends or hang-out buddies, I'd see myself engaging in a conversation like this with him, but like I mentioned before, he and I weren't friends. We weren't enemies either; we just didn't know each other.

On Friday, June had me meet up with him at the hotel. He called my cell phone at about 7:30 to say he'd explain everything when I got there.

I must admit, I was nervous driving through town, but not about getting caught. Like I said before, I had no qualms with the kid. I guess I just couldn't see myself doing such a thing. But once I thought about the money, that changed.

Anyway, we were down near the lobby of the hotel. June passed me a small briefcase covered in a black cloth. I guess I wasn't expecting the money so soon. As senseless as it sounds, I wondered why he would give me the money first. I shortly realized it was the weapon, a sawed-off shotgun. It looked kind of like the gun my dad used for hunting when I was a child.

June began to tell me exactly what was going on and what needed to be done.

"Use these," he said, passing me a pair of latex gloves. "I'll shut off the alarm. But make haste," he said. "I don't know when it will turn on again."

June insisted it had to be done within the hour, as that's about the amount of time it would take before the alarm system would kick back on.

"Take the ruby necklace stashed in the kitchen cabinet. There's also fourteen hundred dollars tucked away in a cup beside a stack of bowls. Take them for your trouble. I want this to look like a robbery." June said that the apparent theft would make the investigators look for a burglar.

As I was about to step away, June pulled me back. "Don't drive," he said. "Ride your bike. Then come get the money. If you have to drive, take your car halfway to the crime scene. Leave as fast as you can. Get off the bike and ditch it somewhere, I don't care. I'll get someone to call the police about twenty minutes afterward. In the meantime, you just focus on getting your money."

On Friday night, things were going according to plan. At least from the beginning they were.

I had the gloves on, and the gun was in my front pocket. I must admit, I was a little nervous—terrified, if you want me to be completely frank.

Breaking in through the back entrance, I heard the sound of shattering glass as it fell to the floor. "Think about the money," I repeated to myself as I stared at my reflection in the glass-fronted china cabinet.

It was hard enough to see in the dark, not to mention trying to see through the black nylons pulled over my face.

I had been in the house for fifteen minutes already—I was timing myself. I quickly reached into the cabinet for the fourteen hundred dollars. Then I went upstairs. There they were, both of them, lying in the bed.

It all happened fast. Three shots spat out of my revolver. Two hit Lavira, and one got Adrian in the spine. I later learned that Adrian had been paralyzed from the waist down and that Lavira had died instantly, as one of the bullets had hit her vertebra.

Damn! I thought, running out the back door and rushing to my bike. *I left the necklace in the house.*

I ditched my bike near a public phone booth.

It started pouring down rain. I shouted, screaming colorful expletives and banging my hand on the glass wall of the phone booth.

"June, what do I do? I messed up."

"Slow down," he said. "Slow down." By the time I made it back to the hotel, the police were already at the crime scene.

All I remembered hearing June say was, "Just stick to the robbery plan." Twice he'd said it.

I was out of breath and still disoriented. June pulled me aside and handed me twenty-three thousand dollars in cash, more money than I'd ever seen in my life. I invested the money in a trust fund.

I had been taught my whole life that if I worked hard, it would pay off. The sad truth is, that's not always true.

It Was an Intense Scream

S o that's when it happened, in my desperate attempt to
get even or to show pure arrogance.

For whatever reason, Dawn brazenly poured the entire
can of oil all over the tall, bodacious body of Angela, literally
soaking her from head to toe. The oil dripped from her face
as she spit the excess from her lips like a child coming up for
air in a swimming pool and spitting out water.

Before I knew it, as if from out of nowhere, Dawn struck
a match. Then she tossed it at Angela. In the blink of an
eye, she took one step back, watching the flames consume
Angela's delicate flesh. Angela let out an intense scream,
panting as if she were running on a treadmill or something.
Dawn laughed hysterically.

Weeks prior, on a hot, thirsty July night, Dave had just
stepped out of Café's nightclub. Sweat dripped from his
body as if he'd just come out of a hot shower.

The soft night wind cooled his forehead, but not enough
to beat the intense summer heat.

Crowds of people slowly swarmed in every direction.
Unfastening his collared shirt, Dave approached a signpost.
He leaned against it to wipe his brow. That's when he
overheard a few girls giggling on the side benches, saying

something to the effect of, "Stop! Go somewhere else. Leave." The small group of girls were complaining.

But Dave was not amused in the least; he seemed to be too preoccupied with his own thoughts to pay any attention to the girls.

Continuing to wipe his sweat, Dave idly drifted in and out of thought.

Suddenly a band of dudes—four, to be exact—slowly approached him, saying, "Stop watching Angie. She says you're giving her problems."

Dave was shocked at what he'd just heard, thinking, *That sounds crazy.* He even turned around to see if there was anyone else nearby. "Perhaps they were speaking to someone else," he mumbled beneath his breath. Looking one of the guys in the eye, he asked, "What—?" But before he could finish his question, the tallest guy pressed his hand into his chest.

"The tall girl with red hair," the guy answered.

Dave didn't know who he was talking about. Shrugging his shoulders, he asked, "What girl?" Within moments, the girl with the red hair stepped out of the crowd, approached him, and stared intensely into his eyes. He thought he'd seen her someplace else before—*perhaps somewhere other than here,* he thought. But nothing came to mind. He started to feel the tension around him increase.

One of the guys came from beneath, pulling Dave to the ground, while the others kicked and punched him. Angie stood back laughing at the whole thing. She seemed to be getting a big kick out of it. The four dudes must have beaten Dave for a good hour and fifteen minutes, easy. When the fight was over, he had blood oozing from his nose. He even had a black eye. Limping on the way to his car, Dave was badly bruised from the kicks and thumps to his head. He could see the girl through his rearview mirror. He thought of her with pure hate.

For whatever reason, Dawn brazenly poured the entire can of oil all over the tall, bodacious body of Angela, literally soaking her from head to toe. Oil dripped from her face as she spit the excess from her lips, like a child coming up for air in a swimming pool and spitting out water.

Before I knew it, as if out of nowhere, Dawn struck a match. In the blink of an eye, she tossed it at Angela. Then she took one step back to watch the flames consume Angela's delicate flesh. Angela let out an intense scream, panting as if she were running on a treadmill.

Blood was still oozing from Dave's nose as he awoke from his horrific fantasy of Angie being severely burned by some lewd character named Dawn. He felt ill knowing he liked someone as terrible as she was, but at the same time he hated someone as beautiful as that tall bodacious girl Angie.

Have you ever imagined doing evil or wished harm on someone? Try being conflicted with the desire to do these things to the same person you have affection for!

About the Author

Rodney Johnson is just a really twisted-up person, but aren't we all? It's like on the one hand, he is extremely shy and passive, the person who is always behind others. On the other hand, he is the quintessential opportunist, a doer who never stops, and an extremely deep thinker. Mix the two and there you have him.

Brain Boxing is a serious confrontation. It's so wrong that it's right. It is influential, hypnotizing, and mind-catching.

People talk about achievements, tending to judge others based on the amount of success they've had. But I write just for fun. If I hadn't figured out how to have my work printed and bound, I'd still be doing something along these lines. But it just so happens that I found a way to market my books and present them to you.

Brain Boxing is my contribution to society.

I'll never apologize for anything I've written. The stories I write take too much time, too much thought. If you don't get them, then someone else will.

Printed in the United States
By Bookmasters